Haunting on a Halloween

FRIGHTFUL ACTIVITIES FOR KIDS

Linda White

Illustrations by Fran Lee

Gibbs Smith, Publisher
Salt Lake City, Utah

First Edition
06 05 04 03 02   5 4 3 2 1

Published by
Gibbs Smith, Publisher
P.O. Box 667
Layton, Utah 84041

Orders: (1-800) 748-5439
www.gibbs-smith.com

Edited by Suzanne Gibbs Taylor
Designed by Fran Lee
Printed and bound in Hong Kong

Library of Congress Cataloging-in-Publication Data

White, Linda, 1948-
Haunting on a Halloween : frightful activities for kids / Linda White ;
illustrations by Fran Lee.—1st ed.
p. cm.
Summary: A collection of ideas and directions for making Halloween
decorations, costumes, snacks and parties that depend more on
imagination and creativity than on money.
ISBN 1-58685-112-8
1. Halloween decorations—Juvenile literature. 2. Halloween
cookery—Juvenile literature. 3. Halloween costumes—Juvenile
literature. [1. Halloween decorations. 2. Halloween cookery. 3.
Halloween. 4. Costume.] I. Lee, Fran, ill. II. Title.
TT900.H32 W49 2002
745.594'1646—dc21
                                        2001004684

For some of our own princesses,
gypsies, and swamp monsters:
Christie, Sandy, Melissa, Katie, and Katherine
—LW

BOO! For some of my best little friends:
Lena, Jake, Emily, Travis, Roby, and Kaden
—FL

CONTENTS

HALLOWEEN!

The October moon rises in an inky black sky. An owl hoots mournfully from a silhouetted tree branch. The wind blows through naked shrubs. Branches skritch together eerily. A small mouse skitters through dead leaves. A dog howls. The hair on the back of your neck stands on end.

It must be Halloween! And time for spooky fun!

Families across the country have chosen Halloween as a day (and night) to dress up as someone—or something—else, turn down the lights, convert the family room into a haunted house, brave the imagined ghosts and ghouls outside the door, and conjure up some frightfully good treats.

Halloween fun can come from the imagination—not the superstore.

Start by crafting a one-of-a-kind jack-o'-lantern, or create a roomful. Then, transform your door, window, table, or whole room with eerie decorations and designs. Cobble together a unique costume you won't find in any other pumpkin patch.

The crafts, decorations, and activities included in this book can be assembled from simple materials gathered from around the house, the corner store, or local craft store. Most are inexpensive and can be made in an hour or during a relaxed evening by the fire.

Of course, every ghost, ghoul, and vampire needs something to bite into, and you'll find a cauldron-full of tasty recipes to put meat on any skeleton.

Once you've decorated and outfitted and prepared, you'll want to share the holiday with family or friends. If you plan to host a party, you'll find ideas, games, and activities to take you all the way to the "bewitching" hour.

You'll also find Rikki Raccoon throughout with helpful tips.

OOOOOOOOOooooooooooooohhhh, are you ready for some fun? Then rattle them bones and let's get started.

BEWITCHING CRAFTS

ike fall leaves, the bold blacks and oranges of Halloween make a big impact wherever they are scattered. With a bit of imagination, some interesting materials, and a little time, you can transform your desk, your family's dining room table, or your entire front yard into a Halloween haunt. Get a few neighbor kids together and you can change the entire neighborhood with decorations not available anywhere else.

Good decorations start with good designs. Make up your own or use the ones found in this section. See that vacant spot in your room? Let's make something to fill it up—how about a jack-o'-lantern?

Jack-o'-lanterns

The last crop to ripen each fall is the pumpkin. Once the pumpkins turn a dark orange, it's only a matter of time until jack-o'-lanterns, long the symbol of Halloween, light up the night. No matter if your jack-o'-lantern will be big or small, squat or tall, you'll want to choose a good pumpkin.

Picking a perfect pumpkin

- Find a pumpkin in a shape you like.
- Check the pumpkin for bruises—soft, dark spots on the skin. A bruised pumpkin rots quickly, so if you find one with bruises, look for another.
- Check for scars—these are hard brown ridges some pumpkins have. Some may work with your design or you might prefer one that doesn't have any.
- Does the pumpkin have a stem? Does your design need one? If it does have a stem and it comes off, you can always glue or toothpick it back on.
- Make sure your pumpkin has at least one flat "sittin' place."
- Thin-skinned pumpkins let some light glow through the shell, while thick-skinned ones allow light only through cutouts. Which type of pumpkin does your design need?

PUMPKIN-ALITY

	SURPRISED	HAPPY	ANGRY	WICKED	FRIGHTENED
Eyes					
Nose					
Mouth					

Designing appealing pumpkins

Jack-o'-lanterns most often appear with grinning faces cut out in triangle patterns. But sometimes we want something different and there are as many possibilities as there are pumpkins in the patch. Before you start carving, decide on a design (or designs).

Have your design ready before you start carving and ask an adult to help you carve your pumpkin!

BRIGHT IDEA—SAFE LIGHT SOURCES

Candles are great for jack-o'-lanterns but must be watched carefully because of fire danger. Small flashlights and light sticks are safer forms of illumination. Cover the light with either colored cellophane or plastic wrap for an eerie atmosphere. Or, place a string of white electric lights inside the pumpkin or stick each light into holes poked inside the pumpkin's shell.

Carving a pumpkin

You can draw your design directly onto the pumpkin with a marker. (Using a red marker rather than black makes any remaining lines less obvious.) But it's easier to perfect the design on paper and make sure it will fit. You know . . . plan ahead!

Not all pumpkins are carved

No time to carve? Don't like the mess? No helper at home to handle the sharp knife? Paint your pumpkin—or tape it! Bright faces can be painted on pumpkins, squashes, or gourds.

Use poster paints, clean-up-with-water acrylic paints for bright faces, or glow-in-the-dark paints for a face that grins back at you when the lights go out. Reflective tape cut into shapes and stuck onto your pumpkin will also light up a dark corner if there is a smidge of light for it to reflect. Find these glow-in-the-dark items at craft shops.

Seeds, seeds, seeds

Eat some now—plant some later!

Roasted pumpkin seeds

What you need:

2 cups pumpkin seeds
Paper towels
2 tablespoons vegetable oil
1 teaspoon salt
Medium-sized bowl
Baking sheet

What you do:

1. Have an adult preheat the oven to 350 degrees.
2. Rinse seeds in cold water and remove all the pumpkin slime.
3. Spread seeds on paper towels and pat dry with another paper towel.
4. Put seeds, oil, and salt in a bowl and mix until all seeds are well oiled.
5. Spread seeds on a baking sheet in a single layer.
6. Bake for about fifteen minutes or until seeds are crisp and golden brown.

For softer seeds, boil them in four cups of water with a teaspoon of salt for ten minutes between steps two and three above.

For a tasty change:

Add one tablespoon Parmesan cheese and/or one teaspoon mixed herb seasoning to oil and salt before mixing with seeds. Or substitute two tablespoons melted butter for the oil, and instead of salt, add two tablespoons brown sugar and one teaspoon pumpkin pie spice or cinnamon.

Plant a Pumpkin Patch

What you need:
- A handful of pumpkin seeds
- Paper towels
- Plastic, self-sealing bag
- A patch of ground that gets lots of sun
- Small shovel

What you do:

1. Wash pumpkin seeds in cold water and remove all the pumpkin goo.

2. Spread seeds in a single layer on a paper towel. Let sit several days or until thoroughly dried.

3. Place seeds in the self-sealing plastic bag and store in the freezer until spring.

4. After the danger of frost has passed (any gardener or garden center will know the average date in your area) and the ground is warm, loosen the dirt where you will plant your seeds. Pumpkins need lots of room!

5. Use a garden fork or a shovel to dig up an area as big as a hula hoop and about six inches deep.

6. Mound the loose dirt back into the hole, leaving a small hill above ground. Add extra dirt if needed.

7. Dig a moat around the edge of the mound six inches wide and six inches deep to hold water that runs off.

8. Plant six seeds in the center of the hill about one inch deep. Press soil down firmly.

9. Water gently. When you can stick your finger an inch into the mound and feel no moisture, water again.

10. When seedlings are about four inches high, thin the plants by pulling out the weakest ones, leaving the three strongest.

11. Pull weeds from your patch regularly or they will take your pumpkins' food and water.

12. Tend your plants all summer. In hot weather, you will have to water your pumpkins often.

13. When pumpkins turn orange, cut from vine.

14. Carve a crowd of jack-o'-lanterns.

Designs

These designs add a "spooktacular" atmosphere wherever you use them. Shrink or enlarge designs (see pages 18-19 for instructions) as needed. Use them in the projects you'll find on the following pages, or let loose your imagination! Decorate a sweatshirt, make place mats and place tags, chair-back covers, window scenes, pillows, Halloween wallpaper . . . What will you decorate?

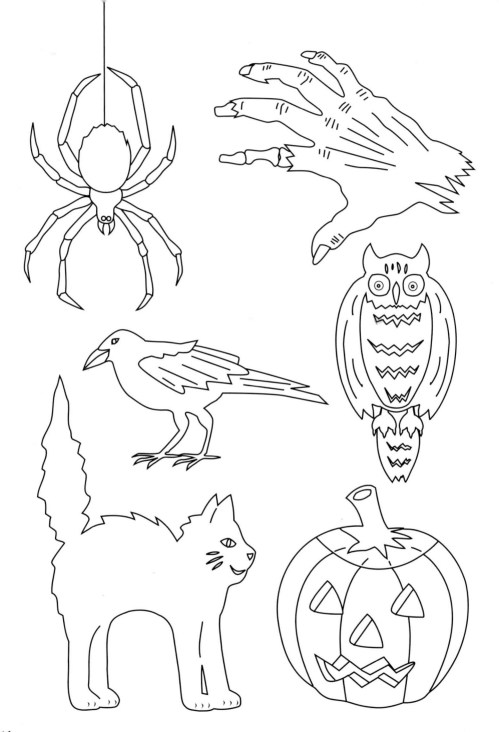

BRIGHT IDEAS

BEWARE OF BATS!

Use glow-in-the-dark paints or markers to outline any design. Add details to make a shocking sight after the lights go out!

Sizing designs

Have you found a design you want to use but it's not the right size? There are ways to make it bigger or smaller.

- Eyeball it! Draw the size you need on a sheet of paper just by looking at the original design.

- Enlarge or reduce it on a copy machine or a scanner. Then you may enlarge or reduce the new copy to get to the dimensions you need. Ask someone who knows how the machine works for help.

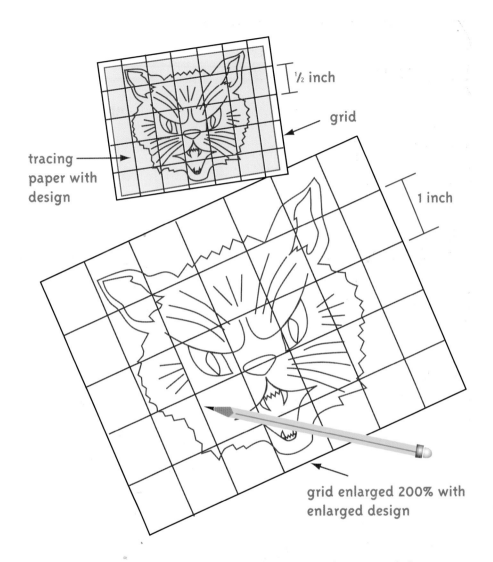

½ inch

grid

tracing paper with design

1 inch

grid enlarged 200% with enlarged design

● Use a grid. Make a grid of squares that covers the original design on a square sheet of tracing paper. For a small design, make them half inch by half inch; for a larger design, make them one-by-one-inch square. Make about five squares in each direction. Place the grid over the design. Now enlarge the grid on another piece of paper. Make the same number of squares. If you want to make the design three times bigger than the original, make the squares three times bigger. Draw the same design lines in the larger squares as you see in each of the smaller ones.

Designing projects

Here are some spirited project ideas to get you started.

Bats at Ya'

Drape the corner of a room with a flock of bats shrieking from their cave. Hang them away from the traffic so people won't be bumping into them. It might make them batty!

What you need:

Bat pattern from page 15 or 18

Black construction paper

Wooden paint stirrers (from a paint store) or strips of wood (called laths) or quarter-inch dowels (from a lumberyard)

Black paint

Nylon thread or fishing line in varying lengths
(twelve to thirty inches)

Scissors

Tape or thumbtacks

Glue

What you do:

1. Paint both sides of paint stirrers, laths, or dowels with black paint.

2. Enlarge the bat pattern several times, making several sizes of bats from small to really large.

3. Cut bats out of black construction paper. You may need to tape several sheets together for the larger bats.

4. Tie a piece of nylon thread or fishing line to the center of the wood piece. Glue or tape the stick along the bat's spine. The stick will be on top of the finished bat when hung from the ceiling.

5. Tape or thumbtack the free end of the line to the ceiling. Be sure to get permission to do this from your adult helper.

Silhouettes

A silhouette is a shadow, stopped dead in time. It is the dark outline of a person or thing that forms when they stand between you and a bright light. Their sizes and shapes are different from the actual people or objects—distorted . . . spookier. You can cut silhouettes out of black paper and plaster them all over your windows, doors, and walls.

On windows:

Light playing through a window filled with silhouetted jack-o'-lanterns, bats, or spiders will startle visiting trick-or-treaters. Use black construction paper and the designs on pages 15 to 17 to create silhouettes. Tissue paper taped across any openings in the designs adds glowing color and haunting appeal.

On doors and walls:

Light doesn't shine through walls and solid doors but you can still make shadowy silhouettes for them. Enlarge the black cat pattern on page 16. Cut it out of black construction paper. Glue it to a big, yellow, full moon rising over an old fence. Glue your entire design onto a sheet of dark blue paper. Maybe you'd prefer a witch on a broom, or a mad scientist mixing a foul concoction under the yellow glow of a hanging light, or a trio of ghosts trailing along the hillside. Place them beneath the branches of a big tree against the light of the full moon! Use one of these ideas or come up with your own.

Design your own silhouettes:

Tape a large sheet of newspaper, butcher paper, or craft paper to a wall (after asking permission). Shine a bright light onto the paper. Ask a friend to stand between the light and the wall in a menacing pose. Move the light or the friend to different places until the silhouette is the size you want it. Have your silhouette carry a lantern, a big ring of keys, or a shovel. Trace around the shadow onto the paper on the wall, then transfer that pattern to black paper. You may need to tape several black sheets of paper together to get a piece large enough for your design. Cut out your shadowy friend and ask permission to tape it to a wall or door. Masking tape is safest for paint and other wall finishes.

Ghastly Lantern Gang

Gather some glass jars and turn them into a glowing or glowering bunch of Halloween lanterns sure to chase away any unfriendly spirits.

What you need:

Glass jars of different sizes

Tissue paper—orange, yellow, green, and black are good choices

Small candles with flat bottoms (tealight candles would work well)

Ruler

Pencil

Tape

Long matches

Scissors

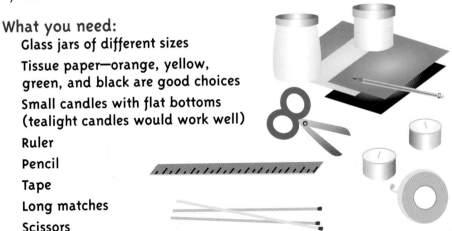

What you do:

1. Use the ruler, pencil, and scissors to cut a piece of tissue paper to fit each jar.

2. Draw a face on the paper and cut out the pieces where you want light to shine through.

3. Tape the paper around the outside of the jar. You may want to add a second sheet of paper behind the cut-out ones. The cut-out holes will glow in the second color.

4. Place a candle in the bottom of each jar.

5. Arrange your jars around the middle of a table, cluster them on a counter or dresser, or line them up on a porch rail.

6. **DANGER!** Ask an adult to light the candles, and do not leave them unattended!

Want something besides a face? How about a fluttering bat or a yellow moon and stars?

Express lanterns

Draw a spiderweb and spider onto the paper with a black marker before taping it to a jar. Or stick Halloween stickers with recognizable silhouettes (outlines) on the jar before taping on the paper.

Chilling place mats

Wouldn't you enjoy serving your Halloween meal on place mats made for the occasion?

What you need:
Craft paper or brown paper bags in 12-inch by 18-inch pieces
Construction paper
Glue
Scissors

What you do:

1. Enlarge your favorite designs from pages 15 to 17 to fit the twelve-by-eighteen-inch background. Cut them out of construction paper.

2. Add some of your own details, like a big yellow moon and a picket fence to a black cat place mat. Use midnight blue paper rather than the craft paper as a background for swooping bats. Cut out a tree limb for the owl to perch on. What else can you think of?

3. Glue your scene onto a piece of brown craft paper (about twelve inches tall and eighteen inches wide) or onto the front or back of a brown paper bag.

A bedsheet bought at a secondhand store would make a great tablecloth! Dye it the color you need with help from an adult. (You could even add tattered or frayed edges.)

Tombstone chair backs

These tombstones will hold your place . . . until you're ready.

What you need:

A paper bag or old pillowcase for each guest's chair
Black marker

What you do:

1. Draw a skeleton, skull, or witch with wings on each bag or pillowcase.
2. Write a tombstone saying on each and include your guest's name.

   Here lies Russell

   R. I. P. (Rest In Peace) Heather

3. Drape each "tombstone" over a chairback.

Frightful paper chains

Ghosts and ghouls and witches all in a line . . . oh my! Hang these paper cutouts across the tops of walls or doors, high across a room, or around the edge of your Halloween table.

What you need:

Paper in the color and length needed for your project. Tape or glue sheets of paper together to get the right length or use long strips of crepe paper.

Scissors

Optional:

Markers

Glitter paint

Paint

Cut on dotted line

Do not cut on fold

Do not cut on fold

What you do:

1. Fold a long sheet of paper, six to eight inches tall, backward and forward accordion-style. The folds should be the width of your design.

2. Draw the design on one side of the folded paper. Make sure the design includes connecting sections at the folded sides or you'll end up with single pieces rather than a chain.

3. Cut out along design lines, remembering not to cut through the part of the design at the fold.

4. Decorate with paint, markers, glitter, or whatever you think of, and hang up your chain!

Black cats, ghosts, bats, jack-o'-lanterns, and witches on brooms are all great choices for Halloween chains. What will you make?

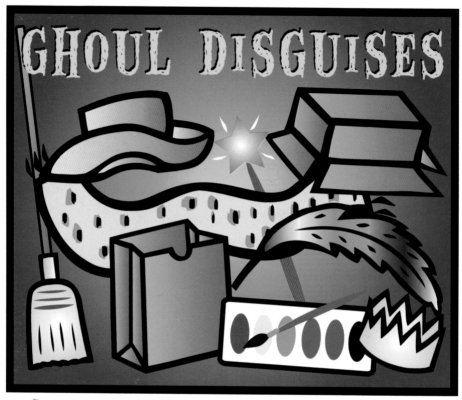

GHOUL DISGUISES

Making a costume can be just as much fun as wearing one. No need to spend lots of time or money—after all, you may only wear it once. Use that magic ingredient—imagination. Find things around the house you can use. Mix them up a bit, add a hat, some props, a little face paint, and . . . presto, you're some-one—or something—else for the night.

What do you have?

Do you have a long-sleeved shirt or sweatshirt?

. . . some paper bags?

. . . a box?

. . . a hula hoop?

IMPROVISE means "to create using materials you already have."

What do you need?

- Make a long black skirt from a trash bag or crepe paper by cutting the length you need, gathering and taping to fit around your waist. Tatter and stretch the bottom edge for added effect.

- Every superhero, witch, and vampire needs a cape. Enlarge this pattern to fit. Cut the pattern from a trash bag, old sheet, or piece of felt. Add a necktie using elastic, Velcro, or string, and decorate your cape with shapes or emblems using stickers or scraps of material.

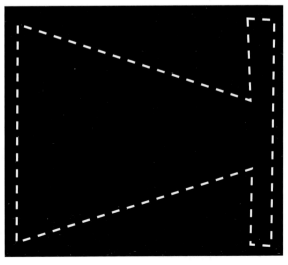

● Hat for a witch, a wizard, or a princess or a dunce!

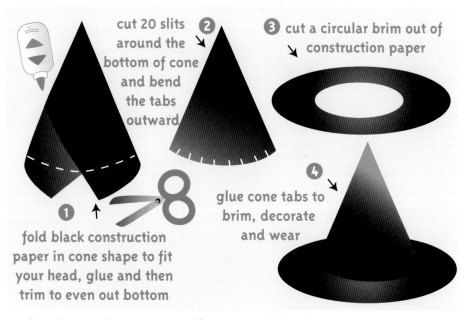

cut 20 slits around the bottom of cone and bend the tabs outward

2

3 cut a circular brim out of construction paper

1 ↑
fold black construction paper in cone shape to fit your head, glue and then trim to even out bottom

4 ↘
glue cone tabs to brim, decorate and wear

● Make cat, bat, or werewolf ears out of fake fur or construction paper and attach them to a headband of the same color.

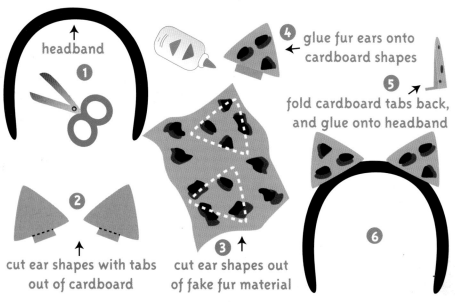

↑
headband

1

4 glue fur ears onto cardboard shapes

5 ↗
fold cardboard tabs back, and glue onto headband

2
cut ear shapes with tabs out of cardboard

3 ↑
cut ear shapes out of fake fur material

6

Face painting

Take a couple colors of face paint, add some practice and imagination, and you can turn yourself into one of thousands of different characters—grinning or growling. Caution! Face paints can be messy. Take care not to get them on good clothes. Have paper towels or rags handy for cleanup.

What you need:

Face paint—either bought or made at home (see recipe on following page)

Sponge for blending colors and painting face

Cotton-tipped swabs for soft or broad lines

Paintbrush for drawing fine lines

Glitter solution for added drama

Eyeliner pencil for dark lines and darkening teeth

If you don't have the color you need, you can mix colors. You can also add white to make colors lighter, or black to make them darker.

Blue + yellow = green
Red + **blue** = purple
Red + yellow = orange
Green + **red** = brown
Some of each = **black**

Recipes for Disguise

Do all your mixing in the sink where cleanup is easy and spills go down the drain. Warning: food coloring dye can stain—you, your clothes, the carpet, and even the sink. Ask permission from your adult helper before making any of the following recipes.

Face Paint

What you need:
1 teaspoon cornstarch
$\frac{1}{2}$ teaspoon water
$\frac{1}{2}$ teaspoon cold cream
Food coloring

What you do:
1. Mix the cornstarch and cold cream together.
2. Stir in the water.
3. Add drops of food coloring, one at a time, mixing well after each drop until you get the color you want.

Need larger amounts of paint? Mix one part shortening with two parts cornstarch. Color with small amounts of food coloring.

These face paints can be removed with soap and water.

Fake Blood

Some disguises just aren't complete without a few drops of "blood." Follow the directions below to make your own. Again, ask your adult helper first.

1. Pour small amount of clear corn syrup (the same amount you will need for "blood") into a small bowl or squeeze bottle.

2. Add red food coloring, mixing after each drop, until you get the color you want.

3. Apply with a brush, or dribble from bottle.

Scars, Warts, and Scabs

1. Make a deep scar by putting a thin line of rubber cement across a fleshy area of skin—your cheek, arm, or thigh. (Before you do this, put a small drop of rubber cement on the inside of your arm to make sure you aren't allergic to it.) When the cement is dry, pinch skin on either side of line around it. If you like, add a bit of fake blood to the deepest area of the "scar." The scar can be rubbed off later.

2. To create warts and scabs: mix 1 teaspoon flour, 1 teaspoon water, and 1 teaspoon corn syrup. Mold a small amount into the shape of a wart and stick it on. Want a yucky scab? Add a bit of oatmeal or other grainy cereal and a drop of red food coloring.

THE MANY FACES OF HALLOWEEN

WITCH
Paint face green
and lips black
or red. Add moles.
Wear a wild-haired wig,
or have an adult help you
spray color onto your hair.

SKELETON
Paint face white
and add black details.
Wear a black turtleneck and
black scarf around head.

DRACULA
Paint face white. Add
black details including
widow's peak, arched
eyebrows and lines
around the eyes. Use styling
gel to slick hair back or in
spikes. Wear glow-in-the-
dark wax Dracula teeth,
and paint red blood
dripping out of your mouth.

CAT
Paint whiskers white or
black and paint a pink
triangle nose. Wear a
decorated mask
and cat ears.

GHOST
Wear a sheet over
your head and cut out
three holes for seeing
and breathing.

RACCOON
Paint face using
black and white paint
around eyes and on nose.

Bringing home the loot

Sometimes an ordinary pillowcase or plastic bag just won't do. When the sun goes down and you're costumed and ready to trick-or-treat, you'll be glad you made a treat collector ahead of time.

Trick-or-Treat Bags

For a quick and out-of-the-ordinary trick-or-treat bag, enlarge one of the patterns from pages 15 to 17. Cut the design out of construction paper. Center it on a solid-colored shopping bag, glue it down, and you're ready to haul your treats home in style.

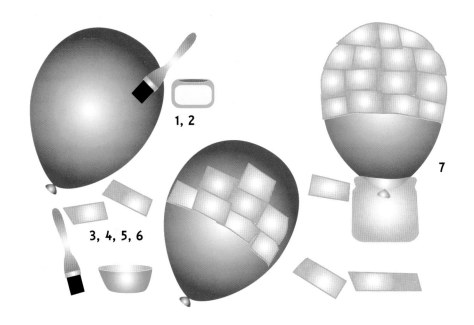

1, 2

3, 4, 5, 6

7

Smilin' Jack Treat Bucket

Start making this papier-mâché pumpkin at least a week before you need it. It needs time to dry.

What you need:
Medium-sized balloon
Newspaper
Flour
Black and orange paint
Paintbrush
Heavy black cording or shoelace—about 20 inches long
Petroleum jelly

What you do:
1. Blow up the balloon and tie it.
2. Spread petroleum jelly on the balloon.

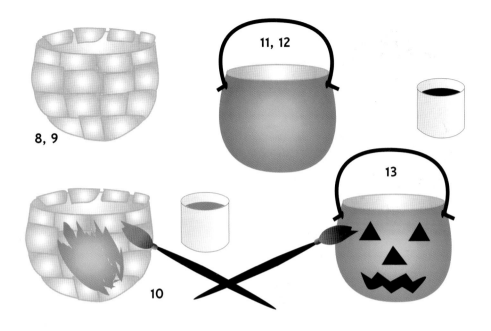

3. Tear long strips of newspaper, three-to-four inches wide.

4. Mix flour and water together for a thick paste.

5. Put each newspaper strip through the paste, squeezing excess out between fingers.

6. Cover the top of the balloon (opposite the knot) with six or seven layers of newspaper, stopping strips an even distance from the knot all the way around.

7. Set balloon on a pail or jar and let dry for two days.

8. When the paper is dry, pop the balloon.

9. Add more strips around and over the rim to make a nice finished edge.

10. When the paper is dry, paint your treat bucket orange.

11. Poke two holes into each side of the bucket about an inch below the rim.

12. Thread cording or lace through holes and tie it for a handle.

13. Use black paint to add a face to one side of the bucket.

14. Fill with treats!

GOBLIN GRUB AND GOODIES

Halloween food can be as spirited as the rest of the evening, whether you serve it just to family or to party spirits. Here are some recipes for howling good treats and hauntingly memorable meals.

Snacks

Coffin Spikes

(No cooking required)

Whenever possible, choose items in Halloween shapes and colors.

What you need:

Wooden kebab sticks or skewers

Package of miniature marshmallows

Gummy worms or other Halloween gummy candies (bugs, witches, monsters, etc.)

Other soft candies such as candy corn, black licorice, gum drops, marshmallow creams, and caramels, that can be pushed onto a stick—choose a variety of colors and shapes

One small pumpkin or apple

What you do:

1. Set aside your favorite candies to decorate spike tops.
2. Thread about ten candies and marshmallows onto each skewer.
3. Stick all skewers into the sides of a pumpkin or apple for display and serving.
4. Poke one of the candies you set aside onto the top of each skewer.

Crunchy Munchy

(No cooking required)
Makes 6 cups

Here's a colorful twist on an old favorite.

What you need:
One cup each:
Pretzel sticks
Roasted pumpkin seeds
Square corn cereal such as Chex
Peanuts
Flavored bagel chips or other
crispy toasted-bread chips
from your grocer's deli section
Candy corn

What you do:
Mix it all together in a large bowl or plastic jack-o'-lantern and serve.

Make a Handy Snack—leave out the pretzel sticks and serve Crunchy Munchy in clean plastic gloves. Find clear gloves at a beauty supply store. Put a candy corn in the bottom of each finger and thumb to serve as fingernails. Fill glove with mix and tie top with bread ties or rubber bands.

Finger Food

(No cooking required)
Makes 8–12 fingers

Aren't you just itching to try this?

What you need:
   1 package cooked hot dogs
   1 red or yellow bell pepper or onion
   1 small jar cream cheese spread—any flavor you like
   Ketchup or cocktail sauce for dipping

What you do:
   1. **DANGER!** Slice one end off each hot dog (your pet dog might like these tiny pieces). The remaining lengths are the fingers.
   2. Cut a shallow slit from side to side across the top of each hot dog, one inch from the cut end. Make another slit an inch below the first.
   3. Cut the pepper or onion into pieces, about 1/2 inch wide by one inch long. These will be fingernails. You'll need one for each hot dog.
   4. Spread cream cheese on the back of each "fingernail."
   5. Stick fingernails to uncut ends of "fingers."
   6. Pile fingers on a plate and point them toward your guests.

Uncanny Pumpkin Bread

(Baking required)
10 servings

Baking bread in a can. What fun!

What you need:

- 1 egg
- 1 cup honey
- ½ cup vegetable oil
- 1 cup cooked pumpkin, fresh or canned
- ⅓ cup water
- ¾ cup flour
- 1 teaspoon baking soda
- ¾ teaspoon salt
- ½ teaspoon cinnamon
- ½ teaspoon nutmeg
- 1 (32 oz.) can or 2 (16 oz.) cans, empty and cleaned

What you do:
1. Mix together first five ingredients.
2. In another bowl, mix together next five ingredients.
3. Carefully pour the bowl of dry ingredients into the bowl of wet ingredients. Mix all together thoroughly.
4. **DANGER!** Pour batter into greased can or cans, being careful not to cut yourself on the top edges. You can cook the bread in a loaf pan if you prefer.
5. Bake at 350 degrees. Bread is done when a toothpick inserted into the center of the bread comes back clean—45 to 55 minutes for the large can, 30 to 35 minutes for the small one.

Variations:

Add ½ cup raisins, ½ cup chopped walnuts, or ¼ cup of each before pouring mixture into can.

Main dishes

Peter, Peter, Pumpkin-Eater Casserole

(Baking required)
4 servings

What you need:

- 1 1/2 cups stuffing mix
- 1 cup chopped chicken, cooked or canned
- 1 tablespoon melted butter or margarine
- Dash of salt
- Dash of pepper
- 1/4 cup chicken broth or water
- 1/4 cup Parmesan cheese
- 1/8 cup Parmesan cheese (for topping)
- 4 small pumpkins
- 1/2 cup water

What you do:

1. Cut tops off the pumpkins as you would if making a jack-o'-lantern.
2. Scoop out seeds and stringy stuff.
3. Set pumpkins in a baking dish and set them aside.
4. Mix top seven ingredients together in a medium-sized bowl.
5. Stuff each pumpkin with the mixture.
6. Sprinkle remaining cheese over tops of pumpkin casseroles.
7. Pour water into bottom of baking dish.
8. Cover pumpkins with pumpkin tops or foil.
9. Bake at 350 degrees for 45 minutes.

No pumpkins? Cook the same mixture in a small baking dish. Omit the last addition of $1/2$ cup water.

Serve with a salad and enjoy.

Scary Pizza

Makes 1 large pizza or 6 individual-sized ones

These pizzas are fun to serve but even more fun to make. Why not let your guests make their own kooky creations?

What you need:

Pizza sauce (See recipe on following page)

Pizza dough for crust (See recipe on page 46)

3 cups cooked ground beef or 2 cups pepperoni slices (if desired)

4 cups grated mozzarella cheese

DANGER! Vegetables cut in weird and wacky shapes to make horns, fangs, eyeball(s), spiky hair, eyebrows, forked tongues, and more.

Preparation:

Make the pizza sauce (recipe follows) and set aside.

Mix the pizza dough (recipe follows). Refrigerate until ready to use.

(Or if you prefer, buy pizza dough mix and canned pizza sauce.)

Wash and cut up vegetables.

Cook the meat.

Making the Pizza:

1. Preheat oven to 400 degrees.
2. Put dough on pizza sheets or two layers of heavy-duty aluminum foil. Use all the dough for a large pizza or shape it into six equal lumps for smaller ones.
3. Using your fingers, press dough toward edges of pan or foil. Pinch edges into a ridge.
4. Pour pizza sauce over crust. Using the back of a spoon, spread the sauce so it covers all the dough except the ridge.
5. Sprinkle meat evenly over the sauce.
6. Sprinkle cheese over the meat and sauce.
7. Arrange vegetable pieces over the cheese to make silly, menacing, or goofy faces.
8. Bake pizza for 10 minutes or until crust is golden brown.
9. Admire pizzas, then gobble them down.

Pizza Recipes

Pizza Sauce:
What you need:

    1 (12 oz.) can tomato paste

    3 cups water

    2/3 cup olive or vegetable oil

    2 teaspoons garlic powder

    1 tablespoon dried oregano

    1 tablespoon dried basil

    2 teaspoons salt

    1 teaspoon ground black pepper

What you do:

1. Mix together tomato paste, water, and oil.
2. Add remaining ingredients and mix well.

Pizza Dough:
What you need:
- **6 cups all-purpose flour**
- **2 cups milk**
- **¼ cup baking powder**
- **1 teaspoon salt**
- **1 cup shortening**

What you do:
1. Mix all ingredients together in a large bowl. Refrigerate.

Turn pizza decorating into a contest for your party. Popcorn and apples complete the meal.

Pizza Decorations:
What you need:
A variety of vegetables cut into different shapes. Vegetables for spooky effects could include onions, peppers (red, green, yellow and/or orange), green onions, olives, carrots, celery, cucumber, zucchini, and corn kernels.

What you do:
1. Wash and dry vegetables.
2. **DANGER!** Cut vegetables into strips, slices, squares, and rectangles to make pizza face details. Remember, let your imagination loose. What can you think of? How will you make it?

Desserts

The Worms Crawl In, The Worms Crawl Out

(No cooking required)
4 servings

What you need:
- 1 cup gummy worms
- 1 (5.9 oz.) package chocolate instant pudding mix
- 3 cups cold milk
- 1 cup Oreo cookie crumbs
- ⅛ cup Oreo cookie crumbs (for topping)
- ½ cup miniature marshmallows
- Graham crackers or cookies for tombstones
- 1 tube of icing with decorator tip for writing
- 4 clear plastic (8 oz.) drink cups

What you do:
1. Set cups on a cookie sheet to catch any drips.
2. Stir chocolate pudding mix into cold milk until well mixed.
3. Stir in one cup of cookie crumbs, miniature marshmallows, and all but two gummy worms.
4. Spoon mixture into cups and smooth top of mixture.
5. Refrigerate until ready to serve.
6. Write names or sayings (R.I.P. [Rest in Peace], Boo, etc.) on the "tombstones."
7. Five minutes before serving, remove cups from the refrigerator. Sprinkle ⅛ cup cookie crumbs over the top of each pudding cup.
8. Pinch remaining gummy worms into pieces and arrange them on pudding tops to look like they are crawling in or out of the "dirt."
9. Set tombstones upright into top of pudding and serve.

Witch Hats

(No cooking required)

What you need:
1 package flat chocolate-striped cookies with holes in the center

1 small bag of Hershey's Kisses

1 tube of orange decorator icing

What you do:
1. Turn cookies upside down so chocolate side faces up.
2. With orange decorator icing, make a line around the outside of the hole in the center.
3. Place an unwrapped Hershey Kiss over each cookie hole.

Spiny Apples

(Stovetop cooking required)
4 servings

What you need:
- 4 wooden craft sticks
- 4 large Red Delicious apples
- 1 (14 oz.) package caramels
- 2 tablespoons water
- Candy corn

What you do:
1. Line a baking pan with waxed paper.
2. Insert one stick into stem end of each apple.
3. In a medium saucepan, combine unwrapped caramels and water.
4. **DANGER!** Ask your adult helper to assist you with this step and the following steps. Cook over low heat, stirring constantly until all caramel is melted.
5. Remove pan from heat.
6. Hold apples over caramel pan and spoon caramel over each one.
7. Place coated apples on the lined baking sheet. Be careful not to drip caramel—it will be very hot and it's hard to clean up.
8. Cut white tips off candy corns. Eat the tips.
9. Press small end of candy corns into soft caramel in spiny ridges from top to bottom of apple.

Kitty Litter Cake

(Baking required)
20–24 servings

Here's the scoop on a cake sure
to get your guests' attention.

What you need:
- 1 box spice cake mix
- 1 box white cake mix
- 1 package white
  sandwich cookies
- 1 (3.4 oz) package vanilla
  pudding mix
- 1 dozen small Tootsie Rolls
- 1 new cat litter pan and scoop

What you do:
1. Make each cake mix according to directions and let cool.
2. Mix pudding according to directions and chill in refrigerator.
3. Crumble small batches of cookies in a blender. Set mixture aside.
4. Crumble both cakes into a large bowl.
5. Add the pudding and half the crumbled cookies; gently mix together.
6. Pour mixture into the clean cat litter pan.
7. Unwrap Tootsie Rolls.
8. Microwave nine of the rolls, a few at a time, until they become slightly soft.
9. Pull on the ends lightly until they are no longer flat. Curve some.
10. Bury them in the cake mixture.
11. Sprinkle the rest of the cookie crumbs over the top of the cake.
12. Heat remaining Tootsie Rolls in the microwave and shape them as you did the others.
13. Roll them across the crumbs on cake top and leave them on top.
14. Serve cake with the new, never-before-used pooper-scooper!

Boo-verages

Clearly Bugged

8 servings

What you need:
24 gummy spiders, flies, worms, and bugs

2 ice-cube trays

1 two-liter bottle of Sprite, 7-Up, or other clear drink

What you do:
1. Place one creature into each compartment of the ice-cube trays.
2. Fill trays with water and freeze.
3. Place three "bugged" ice cubes in each clear drinking glass and pour the drink over them.

Add a quirky clear straw for sipping!

Severed Hand Punch

12 servings

A cold, clammy hand floats in a foul-looking brew.

What you need:
- 1 latex glove
- Red food coloring
- 1 large can frozen lemon-lime drink concentrate
- 1 large can frozen orange juice concentrate
- 3 large cans water (from juice cans above)
- 1 liter ginger ale
- 3 scoops orange sherbet

What you do:

1. The day before: Rinse glove with water before using. Fill the glove with water and two drops of red food coloring. Tie off the wrist end and freeze.
2. Ten minutes before serving, mix lemon-lime concentrate, orange juice concentrate, water, and ginger ale in a large bowl.
3. Add orange sherbet.
4. Cut glove from the icy hand and place the hand in the punch.

Add gummy worms or bugs to the "hand" before freezing.

Once you've carved your perfect pumpkin, decorated your space, and tables are creaking and groaning under the weight of the foods you've made, why not have a party?

Plan the Party

When will the party be? Halloween is always October 31. Do you want to have your party on Halloween night or do you plan to go trick-or-treating? The Friday or Saturday just before or after Halloween could be a good time. Consider things you know you or your guests already have scheduled and plan around them. Do you want an afternoon party or an evening party?

Where will you have the party? A yard, basement, garage, or barn is an ideal place. Each is easy to decorate and there's less worry about food drips and drink spills. A family room, living room, or kitchen might also be a good choice.

How many people will you invite? Most parties are more fun with just a few people. It's easier to do more things and less likely anyone will get out of control.

What will you do? Play games? Have a scavenger hunt? Decorate sandwiches, pizzas, or cupcakes? Have a haunted house? The space you have may determine what you can do. What will you serve? A meal? Snacks? Halloween cookies and punch?

Keep on Schedule

Once you've decided the basics—who, what, where, when, and how—and have written everything down, keep your party on track by planning ahead.

Three weeks ahead:
- Make invitations
- Give party space a good cleaning
- Begin making decorations
- Write a ghost story
- Plan your costume

Two weeks ahead:
- Send out invitations
- Begin making your costume
- Finalize menu and make a shopping list

One week ahead:
- Put finishing touches on your costume

During the week of the party:
- Shop for items on your grocery list (don't forget paper plates, cups, napkins, and plastic eating utensils)
- Decorate

Two days ahead:
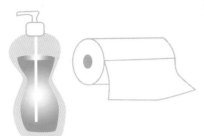

- Do a final cleaning
- Make refreshments that don't need refrigeration

Day before:

- Carve jack-o'-lanterns
- Finish decorating
- Set up any special effects

Day of:

- Set out plates, napkins, cups, etc.
- Make foods that need refrigeration.
- Put on costume
- Paint face
- Set out food

Dim the lights and have a howlin' good time!

You're invited!

Halloween party invitations can be bought but they won't represent you like ones you make yourself! Simple ones can be made using the designs on pages 15 to 17. Just cut them from one color of construction paper in the size you want and glue them onto a construction-paper card.

Make sure your invitation includes important information such as:

- What: A Halloween party, picnic, get-together?
- When: date and time
- Where: address of the party location
- Who is giving the party? (You!)
- Plus any special instructions like: Wear your costume! Bring a treat for everyone to share! Wear your coat, the party's outside!

This information can be written on each invitation or printed on them using a computer.

Games and activities

No party is complete without things to do, and on Halloween, the messier the better! Though today there are few outhouses to tip over like our grand-parents and great-grandparents did, many other Halloween activities they did are still the most fun. Be sure to have prizes on hand for the fastest, the cleverest, and the scariest. Caramel apples and popcorn balls make great awards. Everyone who plays should get a treat.

Bobbing for Apples

Everyone loves playing in water, especially when there's a challenge. Bobbing for apples is certainly that. Fill a large clean tub with water and toss in some apples—at least one per person. The guests take a turn at try-ing to take an apple from the tub. But wait . . . they must keep their hands behind their backs and use only their mouths to capture a floating apple! Everyone and the floor are going to get wet with this one, so be sure to have towels and a mop on hand.

Apples on a String

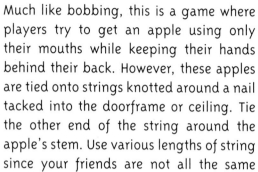

Much like bobbing, this is a game where players try to get an apple using only their mouths while keeping their hands behind their back. However, these apples are tied onto strings knotted around a nail tacked into the doorframe or ceiling. Tie the other end of the string around the apple's stem. Use various lengths of string since your friends are not all the same height. Whoever grabs their apple the fastest gets the prize. If that's too easy, the first to eat their apple down to the core without it falling from the string wins. Some people prefer tying doughnuts to the strings.

Pumpkin Toss

Set five or six different sizes of scooped-out pumpkins in a bunch. Paint a number on each pumpkin—30 on the smallest one, 5 on the largest one, numbers in between on the middle-sized ones. Each contestant stands behind a line on the floor and tosses a beanbag or an unshelled walnut at the pumpkins. Give each person three tries. The one with the highest score wins, but have a prize for everyone. Wax lips might be a good prize.

Make a bean bag by sealing one cup of dry beans inside a sturdy one-quart self-sealing plastic bag. Seal that bag inside another.

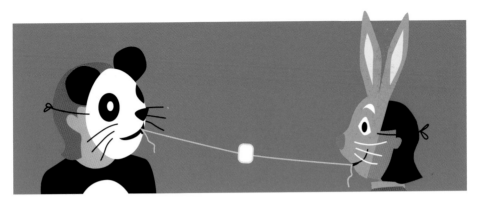

The Marshmallow Gag

Divide partygoers into two-spook teams. Give each pair a marshmallow strung in the middle of a two-foot-long piece of cotton string. Each team-member puts one end of the string in his or her mouth. When the person in charge sees everyone is ready, he shouts "go." Each team member starts "chewing" up the string, pulling it into their mouth until one reaches the marshmallow. Whoever gets there first is the winner! (Don't eat the string!)

Shadow Theater

Tack a white or pale sheet over a doorway and bring your favorite ghost story to eerie life in moving silhouettes. The players perform between a bright light and a sheet, using exaggerated motions and huge, oversized props made out of poster board for the story. The audience sits on the other side of the "curtain."

Decorate Masks

Each guest gets a plain mask or paper plate to decorate. Fill the table with crafty items (glue, markers, elastic, ribbons, feathers, shells, uncooked noodles, buttons, sequins, pipe cleaners, etc.) and turn the artists loose.

Mummy Race

Divide people into two teams and give each team a roll of toilet paper. Tell teams they have five minutes to make the best mummy, AND they have to use the whole roll of paper. At the end of the five minutes, give a prize to the best mummy and something to the other teams, too. Maybe Halloween pencils, popcorn balls, or a clear latex glove filled with treats and wearing a spider ring?

To add more fun to your party, follow these steps to create hair-raising sounds or tell the jokes on the next page.

Haunting sounds

Wind: Fold a piece of waxed paper over the toothed edge of a comb. Place paper-covered comb teeth gently between your lips and practice humming, blowing, and changing the pitch of your voice until you sound like a howling wind.

Rain: Drop bits of uncooked rice onto a metal baking pan.

Thunder: Hold a large sheet of poster board by one edge and shake it.

Fire: Crinkle one or several pieces of cellophane.

Footsteps: "Walk" shoes in a pan of gravel.

Bubbling bog or witch's cauldron: Using a drinking straw, blow bubbles into a glass of liquid. Change sounds by blowing faster or slower and by using a thicker liquid.

Make other spooky sounds by rattling chains, rustling paper, moaning, shrieking, or (chills) scraping fingernails on a chalkboard.

- What's a ghost's favorite ride?
  The Roller Ghoster
- Why are there fences around cemeteries?
  Because people are just dying to get in.
- Why didn't the skeleton cross the road?
  He didn't have the guts to do it.
- What's the favorite game at ghosts' birthday parties?
  Hide and Shriek!

- Why wasn't there any food left after the monster party?
  Because everybody was a goblin!
- How do baby ghosts keep their feet warm?
  They wear BOO-tees!
- What do ghosts like best for dessert?
  Booberry pie with ice scream.

- How do ghosts get to the second floor?
  They take the scares!
- Where do young ghosts go during the day?
  Dayscare centers.
- What do you call a fat jack-o'-lantern?
  A plumpkin.

Other Activity Books from

Gibbs Smith, Publisher

COOKING ON A STICK

Campfire Recipes for Kids
by Linda White
illustrated by Fran Lee
48 pages, $8.95

SLEEPING IN A SACK

Camping Activities for Kids
by Linda White
illustrated by Fran Lee
64 pages, $9.95

HIDING IN A FORT

Backyard Retreats for Kids
by Lawson Drinkard
illustrated by Fran Lee
48 pages, $8.95

FISHING IN A BROOK

Angling Activities for Kids
by Lawson Drinkard
illustrated by Fran Lee
64 pages, $9.95

TREKKING ON A TRAIL

Hiking Adventures for Kids
by Linda White
illustrated by Fran Lee
64 pages, $9.95

WISHING ON A STAR

Constellation Stories and
Stargazing Activities for Kids
by Fran Lee
64 pages, $9.95

Available at bookstores or directly from the publisher.
GIBBS SMITH, PUBLISHER
1.800.748.5439/www.gibbs-smith.com